The Table Football League

"OH, I SAY! HOW DID THAT GET IN? IT SEEMED TO CURL RIGHT OUT OF MACDOUGALL'S REACH! THAT'S AN ASTONISHING STRIKE BY MACKINTOSH! THE CROWD ARE STUNNED INTO ABSOLUTE SILENCE. MANAGER MCTAGGART SHAKES HIS HEAD IN DISBELIEF AND I'M NOT SURPRISED! THAT HAS GOT TO BE THE GOAL OF THE SEASON SO FAR! And there goes the half-time whistle now. I can't wait to see a replay of that in the studio – over to you, Liam!"

Also by Chris d'Lacey:

Henry Spaloosh!
The Snail Patrol

Chris d'Lacey

Illustrated by Philip Reeve

Scholastic Children's Books,
Commonwealth House,
1-19 New Oxford Street,
London WC1A 1NU, UK
A division of Scholastic Ltd
London ~ New York ~ Toronto ~ Sydney ~ Auckland

First published in the UK by Scholastic Ltd, 1998

ISBN 0 590 19983 8

Typeset by
Cambrian Typesetters, Frimley, Surrey
Printed by
Cox & Wyman Ltd, Reading, Berks.

2 4 6 8 10 9 7 5 3 1

For Matthew
and the “5 Live” commentary team!

Introduction

This is Willie Mackintosh, star striker for a little-known football team called Munchester United. Munchester United are one of the teams in the Murton High School Table Football League. They are managed by a boy called Noel Hooper.

Willie Mackintosh is the stuff of table football legend. He has a blob of green paint in his light brown hair and he sleeps in a box with cotton wool padding wrapped around his legs. He is a goal-scorer *supreme*. A dead-ball *specialist*. He takes free kicks, corners, penalties, throw ins, and even goal kicks when things get desperate. He was transferred from Taggart's Tornados at the start of this season for ... a packet of crisps, two sticks of chewing-gum, and a very small tin of tangerine paint.

Well, they do say football is a funny old game...

Chapter 1

The Christmas Present

It all started like this...

One Christmas, Noel Hooper asked his mum and dad if he could have a football shirt with the words "MAN U I LOVE YOU" printed on the back. Noel Hooper is Manchester United mad.

Noel's mum and dad went into a huddle.

"Do you know how much it costs to

put *one* letter on a shirt?" Noel's mum hissed to Noel's dad.

"Fifty pence?" guessed Noel's dad.

"Five quid," said his mum.

"FIVE QUID!" Noel's dad repeated loudly. He looked visibly shaken. His fingers clutched at the arm of his chair as he worked out how much "MAN U I LOVE YOU" was going to set him back. "*Too* much" was the answer he quickly came up with. And that's when he had the bright idea of buying Noel Subbuteo for Christmas instead.

Noel's dad had played Subbuteo as a boy. In his opinion it was the best table football game in the world. On Christmas Day morning he waited excitedly for Noel to open the big rectangular parcel that was sitting in prize position under the tree. Unknown to his father, Noel had shoved that parcel aside, convinced it was a pair of

pyjamas from his gran. A pair of socks, a wildlife book and a chocolate orange were all unwrapped. Then the tension got too much for Mr Hooper.

"That one!" he ordered, pointing grimly at the Subbuteo parcel. "Open *that* one next."

Noel frowned at the prospect of new pyjamas, but to avoid a scene tore the present open anyway. A breathless silence fell upon the room.

"Well, what do you think?" Mr Hooper urged, nervously biting his fingernails.

Noel pushed the wrapping paper aside. "Is it a game?" he asked.

"The best football game in the world," said his dad. "I used to play that when I was your age. Open the box. I'll show you, shall I?"

"Not now you don't," Mrs Hooper said sternly. "*You've* got Brussels sprouts to prepare."

"Oh, blow the Brussels sprouts," Mr Hooper declared, and before anyone could stop him he was down on his knees and clearing a space for the Subbuteo pitch.

"Dad?" asked Noel, as his mum drifted kitchenwards muttering something about "big kids". "If it's called table football, why are we playing down here – on the carpet?"

"The pitch slips about on a table," said his dad, lovingly unfolding the piece of green baize that was marked out just like a football pitch, "unless you nail it down, of course."

"No one's nailing anything to MY table," said a voice from the kitchen.

"Besides it's better on the carpet, Noel. If you want my advice you'll get to know its springiness and all the little tufts."

Noel looked a bit bewildered.

"Home advantage," Mr Hooper

explained, setting out a team of Subbuteo players. "Know your carpet and you'll be unbeatable on it."

"It's important to vacuum it before every match as well," Mrs Hooper piped up hopefully.

But Noel wasn't listening. By now, he had set out his players in a solid 4-2-4 formation and was waiting for his dad to tell him the rules.

"It's just like normal football, really – except you have to move the men about, of course. You flick them at the ball like this." He knocked a man forward with his index finger. The man made contact and the ball moved off the centre spot with a satisfying clack. It rolled up against one of Noel's players.

"Drat," said Mr Hooper, gritting his teeth. "It's your turn now. If the ball hits your men, you get a go."

"That's David Beckham," Noel

beamed, steadily beginning to get the idea. He bent down and flicked David Beckham forward. David rolled the ball sweetly out to the wing.

"Hmph, that was lucky," Mr Hooper sniffed. "You can use your winger now. You're allowed up to three goes with any one man."

Noel flicked his miniature Ryan Giggs into action. Giggs knocked the ball tidily down the line, then clipped it inside the static fullback and angled it into a dangerous position – just behind Mr Hooper's back four.

"Hah, now you've had it," Mr Hooper smirked. "Your nearest man's on the halfway line! You'll never reach the ball from there!"

"Watch this," said Noel, positioning himself behind a midfield player. "And it's Roy Keane..." he commentated, with a deftly-weighted flick that sent the Subbuteo player on a curving, upfield course, "...he makes a surging run from the centre of the park! He runs ... all the way round the blues defenders and ... TOE POKES THE BALL TO THE EDGE OF THE AREA!"

"Flipping heck!" cried Mr Hooper, scrambling to get his goalkeeper into position. But he was far too slow to react to the danger. Quick as a flash, Noel edged around the pitch, leaned down smartly and flicked Roy Keane at the centre of the ball. The ball flew into the top of the net – so hard that Roy Keane went in with it.

"GOAL!" yelled Noel, punching the air in delight. He picked Roy Keane out and gave him a kiss!

"But I wasn't ready!" Mr Hooper protested.

Noel repositioned his men for the kick-off. "You don't have to be ready in the *real* game, Dad."

"Well if you're going to cheat then you can flipping well play with someone else!"

"All right," said Noel.

And he rushed to the phone and rang his best friend, Liam.

Chapter 2

The League

"Really?" Noel exclaimed.

"Honestly," said Liam. "It was my main present. I wanted a mountain bike."

Noel let out a deflated sigh. To his amazement, Liam had got Subbuteo for Christmas as well. Still, now he could play away matches when he wanted to – and so could Liam. His mood brightened again.

"Do you like it?" he asked.

"Like what?" said Liam.

"Subbuteo, dummy!"

"Dunno," Liam answered. "I haven't had a go yet. My dad and my uncle Tony have been playing it all morning, listen..." He held the receiver away from his ear. The sound of angry voices flooded the line.

"*It was NOT offside!*"

"*Yes it flippin' well was!*"

"*You can't be offside if you're not interfering with play!*"

"*That's in real football; this is different!*"

"*Don't be thick!*"

"*Who are you calling thick?*"

"*Well I wasn't looking at the dog, was I?*"

"See what I mean?" Liam cut in. "My dad's a terrible loser."

"So's mine," said Noel. "Do you want a game, anyway?"

Liam sniffed thoughtfully. "We can't

do it here. And I'm not coming to your house 'cos your mum accused me of doing a trump the last time your mad cat went and did a stink."

Noel glanced up. The Hooper's menacing black cat, Slasher, was sitting like an angry shadow halfway up the stairs.

"We could always go to Tim's house," Noel suggested. "His mum and dad make him watch the Queen's Christmas Day speech, so he's bound to be in."

"Good idea," murmured Liam. "I'll ask my dad if it's OK." There was a pause as Liam went back to the front room. "Yeah, that's all right," he said a moment later. "But you'll have to bring your game. Dad's stamped on two of Uncle Tony's players and Uncle Tony has cut up Dad's net with a pair of scissors. See you at Tim's about half-past three."

"OK," said Noel. And he put down the phone.

Tim Weatherspoon lived on the Gladstone Estate, in a five-bedroomed house with a double garage. His bedroom was in the converted loft.

"Never thought I'd be playing my first match at altitude," Liam remarked as he won the toss and chose to play Tim.

"Actually, the house is in a natural valley, Liam. So we're not very far above sea level, actually."

"Actually, I don't care," smirked Liam. "'Cos oxygen or no oxygen, I'm going to beat you 10–0, actually."

"Bet you don't," said Noel, checking his watch and making a bit of a whistling sound. And he was right. At the end of a very scrambled match in which the ball was lost under furniture more often than it was seen in play, Liam had barely managed to scrape a 1–0 victory.

"Yes-ss!" he whooped at the final whistle, punching the air with obvious delight. He lay on his back and did an impression of a dying ant. It was his way of celebrating an "historic" victory.

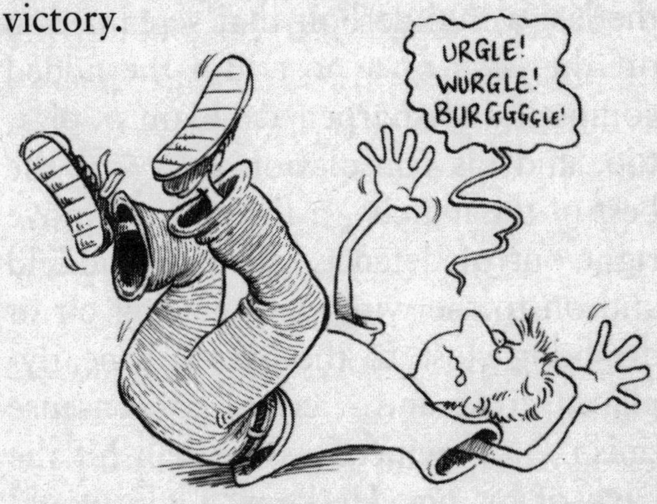

"Huh," Tim sulked, rearranging the players, "anyone'd think he'd won the World Cup."

Noel nodded sympathetically. Liam had only gone in front because Tim's goalkeeper had fumbled madly at a shot and unluckily dragged the ball into his own goal. It was hardly the "fantastic strike" that Liam had claimed.

"I'll put you in your place," Noel whispered to himself. And he did, 3–1, the last a thunderbolt that screamed in off the edge of a post. But the added competition sharpened Liam's play, too, and his consolation goal was the best of the match – a fifteen-flick move right out of defence, through midfield and on to the wing, an amazing bit of dribbling close to the byline, a neatly-placed cross and a crisp, no-nonsense finish. Noel winced as the ball hit the back of his net. He knew Liam would not be such a pushover in future.

After six complete matches, the boys flopped out, exhausted.

"Subbuteo's really ace," drooled Tim. "It's my birthday next week. I'm going to ask Mum if she'll get it for me. Then I'm going to practise like mad. I'm definitely going to beat you next time, Liam."

"No way," said Liam, lying flat on the floor with a teddy for a cushion. "I wasn't even trying when I beat you last time. *Champi-un! Champi-un!*"

"Big-head," Noel muttered and tossed a piece of satsuma peel at him.

"Actually," said Tim, "I think it's impossible to be champion of *nothing*."

"*You're a rotten loo-ser!*" Liam chanted back.

"If we had a proper league, then it'd be different."

"League?" said Noel.

Tim gave a little shrug. "Like proper football. Like the Premier League."

"You need more than three for a *league*, dummy."

"So?" said Noel, giving Liam a kick. "We just find more teams to play against, that's all."

"How?" snorted Liam.

Noel finished his satsuma and got to his feet. "We advertise, *dummy*. Have you got a pen and paper please, Tim?"

Chapter 3

Janice Jumble

"That ought to do it," Noel beamed, pinning up a leaflet on the school notice-board on the first day back of the January term. "I bet we'll get loads of replies from that."

"It's a brilliant advert," Tim agreed.

"It's a stupid advert," Liam grumbled. "What if someone turns up who none of us like?"

"Like who?" said Noel.

"Like ... *her*," groaned Liam, aiming

a finger down his throat as a girl with long brown hair bowled up.

"Hi!" she said gaily. "Happy New Year!"

"Hello, Jumble," said Noel and Tim together.

Janice "Jumble" Sale gave them all a whopping smile. "Hi, Liam," she simpered, tugging his blazer.

"Push off," he moaned.

"So sweet," she said, and cocked her nose imperiously at him. "Anyway, I've come to look at the school notice-board. Stand aside please, Timmy. Ooh, what's this? A Subbuteo league? Ace!"

"You can't be in it!" Liam jeered.

"Why not?"

"You're a *girl*."

"Oh, good, you've noticed." Janice coyly pulled a strand of hair through her fingers. Everybody knew she had a big crush on Liam. Liam winced and started to grind his teeth.

"So, what do I have to do to join, then, Noel?" Janice linked arms and stuck her tongue out at Liam.

"Erm..." Noel began.

"I've got a pitch," she said, casually picking some fluff off his shoulder.

"Honestly?"

"Yep. It's got floodlights, and photographers, and a little bench that the trainer sits on, and corner flags, and a grandstand. Altogether I've got ... thirteen teams."

"Thirteen?" Tim gasped. "Have you got Brazil?"

"Brazil *and* Uruguay."

"She's lying," said Liam.

Janice blew him a pouty kiss. Liam shuddered and wrinkled his nose. Janice tightened her grip on Noel's arm. "My dad's the manager of Murton Athletic. He uses Subbuteo to work out tactics. I've been playing it since I was six years old. I'm quite

good, you know. But if you're all too scaredy to be beaten by a girl..."

"Let's vote," said Tim. "All those in favour of Jumble being in?" He raised his hand. So did Noel.

"Oh, what?" cried Liam, opening his arms. "I'm not playing round at her house. There'll be boy-traps everywhere."

Janice unhooked her arm and hurred on her nails. "I can't imagine *what* you mean, Liam Watts. Anyway, I've been voted in now, so TOUGH. I s'pose we have to make up our own team names and paint our own strips and everything, Noel?"

"Err ... yes," said Noel. He hadn't thought about that. Paint your own strip. That was a good idea.

"And we'll be playing home and away ties, of course?"

Noel glanced at Tim. "It's a proper league," said Tim.

"And we'll be keeping to the Subbuteo rules, I *hope*?"

"Course," shrugged Noel, making a hasty mental note to read the rules properly as soon as he got home.

"And what's the prize for the winner?"

"Your stupid head on a stick," grumbled Liam.

Janice folded her arms. "That's impossible as I'm going to *win*, Liam Watts. But I tell you what, if *you* win, you can take me to the pictures. How's that?"

"Shove off!" barked Liam.

Janice stuck out her tongue.

"There's a trophy in my game," Noel interrupted quickly as Liam lunged forward and Janice darted for cover.

"Great," Janice said over Noel's shoulder, "that'll look good next to my netball medals. Bye-ee!" She dibbled her index finger as if she was flicking a

Subbuteo player then skipped up the corridor singing the "Match of the Day" tune.

"Great," Liam tutted. "Now you've done it. We're gonna look right plonkers playing against *her*."

"She's very confident," Noel remarked.

"Confident? She's barmy!"

"Do you think she's any good?" Tim asked them both.

Noel stared down the corridor, deep in thought. "Dunno," he muttered with a nervous shrug, "but I hope it isn't me who has to play her first..."

Chapter 4

The Meeting

The only other person to reply to Noel's advert was a ginger-haired Scottish boy called Andy McTaggart. He had joined Noel's class the previous summer and nobody knew very much about him. Like Janice, he had played Subbuteo a lot. But unlike Janice, he didn't claim to be good at it. Noel wasn't sure he entirely believed him and marked Andy down as a bit of a dark horse. He was secretly glad when it later turned out that Andy was the one who was drawn to play Janice in the opening fixture.

A week after the advert had gone up on the notice-board and with everybody anxious for the league to start, Noel called a meeting round at his house. The idea, he said, was for all the "managers" to present their teams and discuss the way the league would operate.

"Never mind all that," Liam tutted impatiently. "I want to know who I'm going to be playing. How are you going to work out the fixture list?"

Noel had already thought about that. "In here," he announced, holding up a shoebox, "are the names of all the teams on bits of paper. We'll let my mum draw the first two fixtures. Mu-um!" Mrs Hooper came through from the kitchen.

"Ooh, lovely. I like a lucky dip," she

beamed. She made a big show of stirring up the papers. "And the first one out is ... Taggart's Tornados!" Mrs Hooper showed the paper to everyone. Slasher, curled up on a nearby chair, burbled in annoyance and went back to sleep.

"*Taggart's Tornados*," Tim Weatherspoon whispered into the end of an unpeeled banana.

"... will play ..." Mrs Hooper scrimmaged round for another piece of paper, "Pebble Lane City! Who's that?"

"Me," said Janice. "I live on Pebble Lane."

"*Taggart's Tornados versus Pebble Lane City*," Tim whispered excitedly. "*What a start to the season that's going to be!*"

"Shut up," said Liam, grabbing the banana. "You're giving me the creeps."

"I want to be a commentator when I grow up," blushed Tim. "Me and my dad listen to matches all the time on the radio. They're brilliant."

"Weatherspoon Wanderers!" Mrs Hooper shouted.

"That's me!" whooped Timmy. "First game at home."

"... will play ..." Noel and Liam exchanged tense glances. Which of them was going to be playing Tim?

"Banana Rangers!" Mrs Hooper announced. "Banana Rangers? Who on earth is that?"

"Liam," said Janice. "He likes bananas. Probably explains why he's such an ape."

"Ea-sy," chanted Liam, doing monkey grunts at Tim.

"See what I mean?"

Mrs Hooper nodded. "What about you, Noel? Don't you get a game?"

Noel shook his head. "We've only got five teams in the whole league, Mum, so someone always has to miss a week. The one who misses has to referee the other two matches. Can I have a lift to Andy's house tomorrow?"

"I suppose so," Mrs Hooper nodded and was turning to go when she had a thought: "By the way, what's your team called?"

"Hah!" Liam spluttered. "It's absolutely useless."

"It's better than Banana Rangers," said Noel.

"It's a rip-off," Liam argued. He turned to Noel's mum. "They're called Munchester United."

"Only temporarily," Noel said hotly, "until I can think of something better."

"He's not going to change it," Liam laughed. "I've seen his team-sheet. He's got Ryan *Twiggs* up front, David *Buckham* in midfield and someone called Peter *Schmuckle* in goal. In other words, Manchester United's best players with a few letters changed in their names."

"Shut up," said Noel, turning redder than a cherry.

"He was going to have Olly Gunner Saltcellar as well but that was too silly even for him!"

"Well it's better than Danny Baggage!" Noel snapped.

"Danny Baggage?" Mrs Hooper said, looking confused.

"He's Liam's striker," Janice explained. "Terrible name, isn't it? I can just imagine what the crowd are going to chant when he fluffs a shot in front of goal." She raised her hands above her head and clapped: "*Baggage is a cab-bage!*"

Andy McTaggart spluttered with laughter.

"Shut up," Liam growled. He turned again to Noel's mum. "Ask carrot head to name some of *his* players, then."

"In for a penny..." Mrs Hooper sighed. "Well, Andrew? Who's on the ball for Taggart's Tornados?"

Liam kicked Andy's knee with his heel. "All right," said Andy with grumpy reluctance. "I've got someone called Hamish MacDougall in goal."

"Well, he sounds good," Mrs Hooper smiled.

"And ... Billy McNugget at right back."

Mrs Hooper smiled again. "I think I can spot a Scottish influence here."

"And Robbie MacRobbie in the middle of the back four."

"I can definitely spot a Scottish influence here."

"And MacDoughnut and McLochness and MacNevis," Liam continued.

"They all begin with 'Mc' or 'Mac'," said Noel.

"I think I've got the picture," Mrs Hooper said wearily. "And what about you, Tim?"

"I've got Anasti Ticklikov, Mrs Hooper!"

"Really? Oh dear, you should have said earlier. I've got some medicine in the cupboard for coughs." Tim's face went blank. Noel, Andy, Liam and Janice all began to crease with laughter.

"What's got into you lot?" Mrs Hooper scowled. "There's nothing funny about a tickly cough!"

"Ask him about his chest," Noel giggled.

"Chest?" said Mrs Hooper, looking even more concerned. "Has it got to your chest? Shall I make you up a nice hot-water bottle, Tim?"

Everyone collapsed in fits of laughter.

"They're players, Mrs Hooper. Chestikov and Ticklikov." Tim wrote the names down. "Bulgarian internationals. The finest players in Eastern Europe."

Mrs Hooper made a funny sort of twitching movement. "I see," she said, backing off towards the kitchen. "Well, I'm glad to see everyone's getting into the erm ... spirit of this. We're having tagliatelle for tea tonight, Noel. Erm, that's pasta by the way, Tim, not the name of an Italian footballer..."

"Right," said Noel, regaining command as his slightly dazed mother slipped out of the room. "In my official capacity as league coordinator you all have to read this..." He handed everyone a list of rules he'd typed up and printed on his dad's computer.

Rules of The Murton Table Football League

1. Games will be played to the proper rules as written on the lid of the Subbuteo box

2. There will be no moaning about "proper" football

3. The referee's decision is final and no one is allowed to argue with him (or her)

4. Games will kick off on time and will be

twenty minutes each half (plus injury time)

5. Games may be played at anybody's house but must be on the home team's pitch

6. Dads, uncles and dangerous cats will be banished from the room when a game is on

7. Eating during a match is not allowed as crumbs on the pitch could constitute a serious injury hazard to the players

8. Any player committing three fouls in a match will be sent to his box and will automatically miss the next match

9. Going to the toilet during a match will be deemed time-wasting and ungentlemanly conduct (or, in the case of Pebble Lane City, ungirly conduct)

10. If Liam wins he has to take Jumble out to the pictures

"Rule 10's got to go," Liam snorted at once.

Noel looked at the others. "All those in favour of ditching Rule 10?"

Everybody's hands except Liam's stayed down.

"Rule 10 stays," Noel sniffed.

"That's not fair—" Liam started to protest, but was quickly cut off by Andy McTaggart.

"It doesn't say anything about substitutes. How many are we allowed to keep on the bench?"

"Does it matter?" said Liam, giving Noel a look. "We'll be using the same men, just swapping the names."

Noel ignored him. "I'll make a note about subs. Are we agreed that two is enough?"

Tim and Janice nodded.

"Carried," said Noel.

"Barmy," muttered Liam. "You're all barmy." He dragged Noel's personal

stereo off a chair, popped the headphones on and left the others to it.

"What about transfers?" Andy said.

Noel chewed the end of his pen in thought. "Hmm, I s'pose we *could* have transfers. I might need someone to strengthen my squad."

"Would we swap the actual players?" Tim asked.

"Definitely," said Janice.

"For a fee?" suggested Tim. The others nodded. Andy McTaggart tugged Noel's sleeve.

"I've got a player going cheap, Noel."

"Erm ... well," Noel started. "I wasn't planning on entering the transfer market yet."

"Aw, go on," urged Janice, brimming with excitement, "negotiate with him."

"I've got him here," said Andy. He pulled a Subbuteo player from his pocket and put him on the carpet beside Noel's knees.

Noel inspected the player carefully, then flicked him once or twice around the floor. "Does he spin right?" he said. "He looks as though he might be a bit unbalanced?"

Andy bent down and inspected the surface. "I think that's the tufts in your carpet, Noel."

Noel glanced at the others. They were saying nothing.

"A packet of crisps, two sticks of chewing-gum and ... a tin of that tangerine paint you did that model of a Spitfire in at school, OK?"

"*What?*" said Noel.

"That's his transfer fee. That's what I want for him."

"Bargain," said Janice.

"*But will he go for it?*" said Tim into his imaginary microphone. "*I can tell you the atmosphere is very tense down here at Munchester FC.*"

Noel picked the player up and

examined him again. "All right," he said, shaking hands. "I'll bring you the stuff tomorrow morning."

"Ace," said Andy, looking pleased with himself.

Janice clapped her hands in delight.

"*Fan-tastic!*" Tim gabbled into his mike. "*That's Munchester's record signing this season.*"

Noel gave him a hopeless look.

"That's Munchester's *only* signing this season. I can't afford too many bags of crisps. What is he by the way?"

"Erm ... striker," said Andy.

"He looks it," said Janice.

"What's his name?" asked Tim.

Andy gave a shrug. "Willie ... Mackintosh."

Noel stood Willie Mackintosh on top of his hi-fi. He smiled proudly at his brand-new signing.

"Is it me," said Janice, "or has he got a funny sort of look on his face?"

Noel glanced suspiciously at Andy.

"Trick of the light," said Andy McTaggart.

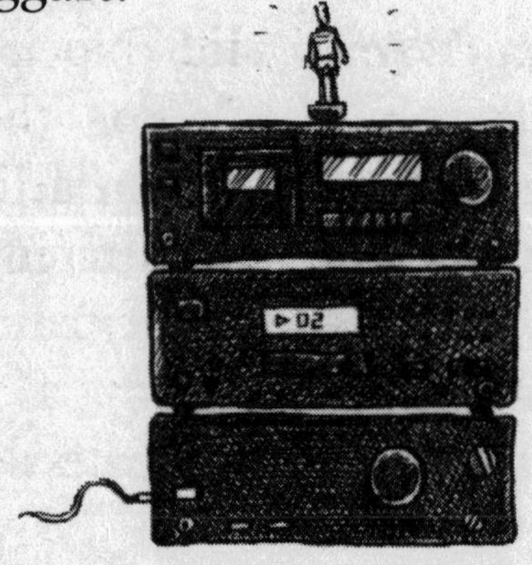

Chapter 5

The Trouble With Willie

"You've been done," said Mr Hooper. "Stitched up. Diddled. You ought to ban that Andy McTaggart from the league."

"Shut up, Dad," said Noel. "I'm trying to concentrate." For the last hour and a half, Noel had been painting the Munchester United team colours on to the all-white team he'd got for Christmas. It was a tricky business that called for delicate movements of the tiny paintbrush. One blob out of place and a player might end up blinded for life. Noel steadied his hand and did a crisp number 11 on Ryan Twiggs's shorts.

So that no one could accuse him of copying the red and white of Manchester United, Noel had invented a completely new strip: dark blue and light blue halved shirts, maroon-coloured shorts and bright green socks. It was a striking combination. He lined his men up on the coffee table in front of him and asked his dad what he thought of the colours.

"They look like they're off to a fancy-dress party!"

Noel didn't care. The Munchester players looked smart, impressive and ready for action. Only one more needed doing: Willie Mackintosh.

"Pass him over, Dad."

"Gladly," Mr Hooper huffed. While Noel had been painting, Mr Hooper had been putting Willie Mackintosh through his paces. He didn't think much of Noel's new signing. "He doesn't spin right," he reported grimly. "Wobbles about all over the place. He's useless, Noel. He can't kick straight. Look, he's got a hairline crack in his legs. I bet he's been broken and glued together at some point. And why is his face sort of globby on one side? He looks like he never recovered from the mumps. You should demand an FA inquiry – get your crisps back at least. You've been well and truly done, I reckon."

"Let me have a go with him," Noel

tutted. He was a bit fed up with everyone having a poke at his brand-new player. It was time to demonstrate how wrong they all were.

"Take a penalty," Mr Hooper said, putting the ball on the spot. He got behind the goal and got ready with his keeper.

Noel crouched down and placed Willie on the "D" of the penalty area. Mr Hooper whistled. Noel launched Willie hard at the ball.

For once, Mr Hooper wasn't kidding. No sooner had Willie left Noel's finger than he started to dip away to the right. He made a reasonable contact with the ball, but the ball did not make contact with the net. In fact, it didn't go anywhere *near* the net. It squirted off over the corner flag, hit the edge of the magazine rack and bobbled away underneath a chair.

"Oh no," said Mr Hooper as a dark shape suddenly shot across the room and began to poot the ball all over the carpet.

"Slasher! Stop it!" Noel protested, luckily managing to catch the ball as it bounced off a skirting-board and into his hand.

Slasher skidded to a confused halt. He looked hard at Noel and hissed like a badly-punctured tyre.

"I should give him that back," Mr Hooper said warily. "You know he doesn't like people stealing his toys."

"It's *my* toy," said Noel. "Mine," he said defiantly into Slasher's face.

Ssss, went Slasher, arching his back. He glanced hawk-eyed at something on the floor. Before Noel could stop him Slasher had pounced on Willie

Mackintosh and was pooting him across the Subbuteo pitch.

"Look out!" cried Mr Hooper as a fierce belt from Slasher's left paw sent Willie flying fast through the air.

"The fish-bowl!" cried Noel. But it was too late. With a plop! Willie landed in the goldfish bowl and sank to the bottom like a deep-sea diver. "Dad, get him out before he drowns!" Noel bleated.

"Or gets gobbled!" Mr Hooper added as a goldfish took a nibble at Willie's ear. Mr Hooper bravely rolled up his sleeve. He dipped into the bowl and brought Willie out with a bit of pond weed wrapped around his base.

Rrrow-oo! went Slasher, looking pleased with himself. He had a quick scratch on the Subbuteo pitch then slinked off towards his dustbin-shaped house.

"That cat is crackers," Noel fumed, drying Willie out on a piece of tissue.

"See what I mean, though?" Mr Hooper said. He nodded at Willie. "Worse than a penguin with two left feet."

Noel frowned and rocked right back on his heels. In all the commotion he'd forgotten about Willie's penalty miss. Secretly, he had to agree with his dad. There was something unnatural about Willie Mackintosh. Maybe it had been a wee bit rash to invest in a player that hadn't been given a proper run-out – or medical. No Premier League manager would have fallen for that. But Noel was far too proud to admit it. "Probably lacks a bit of confidence, that's all. He's under pressure, Dad. New club; new team-mates. Might take a couple of games to settle in."

"He's a crock," said Mr Hooper. "Play him and you'll lose every match."

"That's for the manager to decide," Noel sniffed. And balancing his players on the lid of their box, he went upstairs to get ready for the journey to Andy McTaggart's.

Chapter 6

The First Fixture

"*And you join us here at Budgie Cage Park for the opening fixture in the Murton Table Football League...*" Tim Weatherspoon said, checking the voice level on the tiny tape recorder he had borrowed from his mum.

"Budgie Cage Park?" Liam Watts queried.

Tim's face burned hot. He looked apologetically at Andy and pointed to the pair of caged birds in the window.

"It was the only way I could think to describe your stadium."

"They're canaries," said Andy, a bit perplexed.

"Oh," said Tim and wound back his tape. "*And you join us here at Canary Lane for the thrilling opening fixture in...*"

"He's mental," muttered Liam.

"Ignore him," Janice said kindly to Tim.

Tim smiled and hunched his shoulders forward. "*And the question on everybody's lips is this –* "

"When are you going to shut up?" Liam suggested.

" *– how are Pebble Lane City going to be affected by the luxurious conditions underfoot?*"

To be fair, this *was* the question in Janice Sale's mind. Andy McTaggart's Subbuteo pitch was twenty years old and on loan from his dad. It was

smaller and a darker shade of green than the others and the baize had a deep, luxurious feel. Janice was taking it all in her stride.

"It's lovely velvety turf, Tim," she said, as Tim held the microphone up for a comment. "I'm not certain it'll suit my fast-passing game, but we'll just have to see. If I'm not mistaken there's a bit of a slope towards the Canary Cage end as well. And there's a patch in this corner that looks like it could get pretty boggy should the weather turn bad. Might sap the players' energy late in the game."

"That's where my dad spilled a pint of beer on it once," said Andy, placing a tiny plastic flag at each corner of the pitch.

"Hmm," Janice nodded. "I think I'll tell my players to wear long studs – just for that extra bit of grip on the wings."

Andy McTaggart gave an understanding nod.

"Why have you got orange nets?" asked Noel, examining one of Andy's goals.

"D'you like them?" Andy beamed. "I made them myself from a wee onion bag."

"Spanish onions?" Janice asked.

"Aye, probably," said Andy.

"I thought they looked a bit continental."

On the far side of the room, Liam Watts groaned.

"Did you grunt?" asked Janice.

Liam stuck out his tongue. "Is it me," he said over-loudly to Noel, "or are those three completely stark-staring bonkers?"

"You've got to get your tactics right," Noel shrugged.

Liam closed his eyes and slapped a hand against his brow.

"Gosh, it's breezy," Janice said suddenly. She licked the tip of her flicking-finger and held it up to test the air.

"There's a draught from the kitchen door," Noel noticed.

"*And I have to say conditions are somewhat blustery*," said Tim. "*We could see one or two problems with high crosses today.*"

"Help," groaned Liam, burying his face in a cushion. "I'm locked in a room with four complete loonies."

Noel ignored him and checked his watch. "Five minutes to kick-off. Teams out, please."

Janice opened her Subbuteo box.

"Wow!" said Noel, getting down on his knees to inspect her players. "They're brilliant, Jumble. They must have taken ages to do." Janice's team were painted gold, with a neat red star in the centre of their chests.

Liam leaned forward. Even he looked impressed. "They're better than Taggy's Tornados, that's for sure. Their number 8 looks like he's wearing his shorts right down to his ankles."

"The paint ran," said Andy, going slightly red.

"Why have they all got tangerine heads?"

"It was the nearest I could get to ginger hair."

Liam Watts fell back and hooted with laughter.

"*There's a real North/South feel about this fixture*," Tim said.

Noel checked his watch again. It was 6.59 p.m. He took his referee's whistle out of his pocket and gave a short, sharp peep.

Tim sat up in excitement. "*And yes! The teams are trotting out on to the pitch. Both seem to be adopting an orthodox formation. Referee Hooper tosses a coin and ... Pebble Lane City appear to have won and are electing to play against the slope. The two managers are shaking hands. Nice touch, that...*"

"Huh," Liam muttered. "I'm not shaking hands when *I* have to play her."

"Fine, I'll just sock you in the mouth," said Janice.

"Play," said Noel, and blew his whistle.

"*And the TFL gets under way!*" Tim

roared, and promptly fell backwards off the foot stool he was perched on.

It was fast and furious footballing stuff. It was also the first time that Noel, Liam and Tim had seen the game played to its proper rules. Every time Janice tried to play the ball forward, Andy was allowed a defensive flick. As long as his defender didn't touch the ball or collide with one of Janice's men, he could go on this way, constantly blocking Janice's attacks. Possession changed a lot. At the end of a half which seemed to just flash by in seconds, there had barely been a single shot on goal.

"Phew," gasped Tim, forgetting all about his commentary for a moment. "That was amazing. It's really close."

"It's tight," agreed Janice, getting up to change ends, "especially in midfield, Tim. I don't feel we're distributing the ball out to the wings nearly enough.

But with the wind behind our backs in the second half, I expect us to do a lot better. Cheers."

Tim nodded. He looked at Noel. Noel was exchanging glances with Liam. They both had worried looks on their faces. Some dedicated practising would have to be done before either of them took on Janice or Andy.

The second half began in dramatic style.

"*And the ball is with MacDoughnut,*" Tim chattered, "*probably the Tornados' best player in the first half. He's making a run into Pebble Lane territory. Oh, he's evaded that lunging tackle and knocked the ball into a dangerous position. Here comes McNugget on the overlap! He knocks it through a gap in the Pebble's back four. There's danger here if the cross is pulled back early enough. McNugget is into the area now. A Pebble Lane defender slides across to meet him and ... OH MY GOODNESS! SENSATIONALLY TAKES MCNUGGET'S LEGS! ALMOST KNOCKING HIM INTO TOUCH! THAT LOOKED LIKE A BLATANT PENALTY TO ME AND ... YES! REFEREE HOOPER POINTS TO THE SPOT!*"

"Drat," said Janice, picking up Wilton, her number 5. "I knew it. Didn't change his studs before the game. Useless."

"When you're ready," said Noel, as tense as a rubber band.

Janice put her goalie in the centre of the goal-line.

Andy placed Iain MacNevis behind the ball.

Noel gave a tiny peep on his whistle.

"*MacNevis shoots!*" Tim erupted immediately. "*Crumley dives to his left and makes ... a FANTASTIC save! But*

wait, the ball's come back to MacNevis ... and he makes NO MISTAKE *with the follow-up strike! What an incredible stroke of luck. 1–0 to Taggart's Tornados. Nigel Crumley in the Pebble Lane goal must be ab-sol-ute-ly* GUTTED*!"*

"He is," groaned Janice.

But her disappointment didn't last long.

"*Twelve minutes into the second half,*" gabbled Tim, "*and Pebble Lane City are giving it everything. Taggart's Tornados seem perfectly content to sit back and defend their narrow advantage. But there's a beautiful scything pass from Jefferson. Matthew Cartwright comes to meet it. He tucks it inside to Alan Nicely. Now, what can Nicely do with this? He's going for the one-two with David Rain. And he's got it – off a slightly lucky rebound. Nicely: he takes it round McDuff. He's lining up the shot on his favourite left foot and ... OH YES! THERE IT IS! The equalizer! What was MacDougall thinking then? The ball seemed to squeeze right under his body. 1–1. And I have to say that's been on the cards for some time now."*

"Yes!" whooped Janice.

"Oh no," groaned Andy, cradling his ginger head in his hands. He beat his fist on the carpet in frustration.

"Flippin' heck," said Liam, pulling his collar away from his neck. "I don't think I can bear much more of this. How long to go, Noel?"

"Six minutes," Noel squeaked, completely dry-mouthed.

"*SIX MINUTES!*" Tim repeated frantically. "*Just about time for ANYTHING to happen. The excitement is really spilling into the crowd. The spectators just don't know which way this game is going to go.*"

"Too right," said Liam. "Come on, Jumble."

"Liam!" Janice exclaimed breathlessly, taking her eyes off the game for a moment.

"*And what's happening here?*" Tim Weatherspoon croaked. "*The Pebble Lane defence seems to have fallen asleep!*"

"Are you really supporting me?" Janice simpered.

"Look out!" cried Liam.

"*MacNevis is through! With a clear shot on goal!*"

"Hhh!" gasped Janice, and dived for her keeper.

"*OHHHHHHHHHH, HE'S HIT THE POST!*" screamed Tim.

"Och NO!" cried Andy McTaggart.

"*And the ball's bounced straight back to Cartwright,*" gasped Tim. "*He slots it though to Jefferson, who's fouled by McLochness. Jefferson quickly back on his feet. He takes the kick himself. Taps it to Rain. Rain to Jefferson, back again to Rain.* Great *stuff this by Pebble Lane City. The opposition don't know what day it is.*"

"Come on, Jumble," Noel whispered to himself. He crossed his fingers and leaned a bit closer.

"*Here's Rain, on one of his penetrating runs. Inside to Court. He lays it back to Jefferson. It's a difficult angle! Jefferson shoots! Great SAVE by MacDougall! My goodness, that was close! Corner to Pebble Lane City!*"

"Aw!" cried Liam, throwing back his head.

"*Desperate moments,*" Tim went on. "*Taggart's Tornados are bringing everybody back. The penalty area is heaving with bodies. I can't remember a game quite as tense as this...*"

"Course you can't," said Liam. "It's the first one, you crackpot."

"*Cartwright with the corner. It's a*

good-looking cross, floated high to the far post. The heads go up and... IT'S THERE! IT'S IN THE NET! Pebble Lane have scored in the dying seconds! I didn't see who got it. It might have been Nicely ... yes, I'm getting confirmation from the Pebble Lane bench. It was *Alan Nicely who got the final touch. AND THERE IT IS! The final whistle! Taggart's Tornados 1, Pebble Lane 2. WHAT a dramatic end to this match, and what a gripping start to the Murton High School TFL! I can already see the headlines on the sports pages tomorrow:*

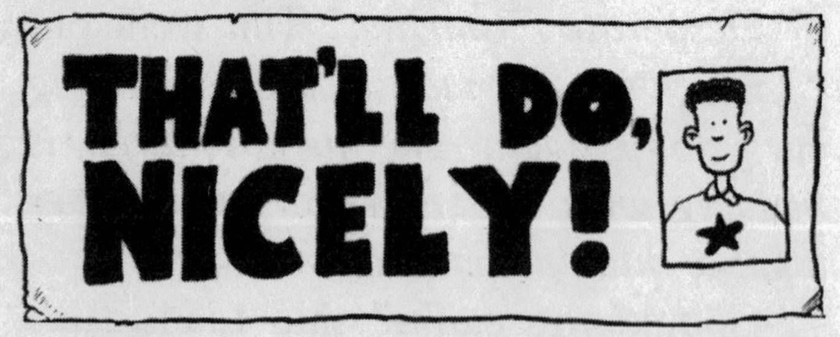

"Ohhh, yes! What an absolute stormer!"

Chapter 7

Noel's Secret Weapon

"Set pieces," Mr Hooper advised, fussily arranging his team of players. "That's where games are won and lost, Noel. Practise your set pieces and you can't go wrong."

"I need to practise more than that," Noel sighed. "Jumble's absolutely magic, Dad. You should have seen her comeback against Taggart's Tornados. It was awesome. Even Liam was totally gobsmacked. Honest, it was mega, mega-brilliant. Janice is just—"

"Shall I kick off, then?" There was a pause. Mr Hooper looked up and frowned. "Noel? Rub that soppy look off your face and let's get started. It was you who said you wanted to practise."

"Umm? Oh, yeah. Sorry, Dad." Noel gave a little whistle and Mr Hooper gleefully kicked off.

"Oh, drat," he moaned, putting too much strength behind one of his flicks and sending the ball out of play for a throw in.

Noel flicked Willie Mackintosh into the centre-forward position. "Dad? Did you ever take a girl to the pictures when you were twelve?"

"I won't bother marking him," said Mr Hooper, jerking a thumb at Willie Mackintosh. "Might need a man on your winger, though..." He

flicked a man back to cover the throw in.

"When did you meet Mum?"

"A-ha!" cried Mr Hooper, as the throw in was a bad one and the ball rolled to the feet of his nearest player. "Brilliantly intercepted!" He quickly tapped it up to his forward line and hotched around the pitch like a demented crab. "Chance here, Noel. You'd better be on your guard!"

"Dad, if you like someone ... a girl, I mean – how do you, y'know, tell them about it...?"

"GOAL!" Mr Hooper yelled with delight. His arms shot up like a couple of rockets and he did a sort of samba dance on his knees.

Noel picked the ball sadly out of the net. Why did he feel so horribly miserable and yet so strangely ... *funny* inside?

"*One-nil*, *one-nil*," Mr Hooper

chanted. "Come on, Noel. Concentrate. I cut through your defence easier than Slasher goes through his cat flap. You'll have to do better if you want to win the league."

That's it, thought Noel. *That's what I've got to do*. "If *I* win the league, Dad, *I'm* going to ask her!"

"Ask who?" Mr Hooper looked completely baffled.

"Doesn't matter," said Noel, and he crouched down for the kick-off.

It didn't take him long to reverse the early goal. In a first half full of non-stop pressure, Mr Hooper's defence was forced into a series of niggling errors. It opened up like a bag of nuts and the Munchester forwards swooped like a set of hungry sparrows. Twiggs knocked one in from the edge of the area. Buckham got another after a dazzling solo run. Twiggs got a third from a scrambled corner. Munchester

United were playing like champions – all except Willie Mackintosh: he was playing like a chump.

"Don't know why you keep passing him the ball," sniffed Mr Hooper, as Noel laid on yet another opportunity for his record buy. Willie had already missed five chances, including one tap-in from the six yard box.

"I've just got to get used to him, that's all," Noel grimaced as Willie walloped the ball behind the goal yet again.

"Face it, Noel. He's an out-and-out duffer. Give him to Slasher. It'll be a quick and painless end."

At that moment, Slasher mooched into the room. He slinked past Noel and jumped lazily on to the arm of the sofa. He peered intently at the Subbuteo pitch. *Rrr-ow-ow*, he rumbled, and gave a fishy yawn. He blinked twice rather aimlessly at Noel, and settled down to bite the nails off his claws.

Mr Hooper hunched his shoulders. "Ooh, I wish he'd go and do that somewhere else. I can't play with him sitting there, *pruning*, Noel. He gives me the creeps. I'm glad I'm not a mouse."

Brr-rup? purred Slasher and twizzled his ears as if "mouse" was a favourite word of his.

Mr Hooper went stiff with fear. "Nice boy," he said, offering the cat a none-too-convincing cheesy grin. "Time to pack up, Noel. You win, OK?"

"Aw, Dad, you're such a wimp," Noel tutted in disgust. "And as for *you*," he muttered, putting a spare ball right at Willie Mackintosh's feet so that even *he* couldn't possibly miss it, "you're on the bench against Taggart's Tornados unless..." Noel stabbed his finger at the out-of-form player.

A-rowww! went Slasher, jerking his head to follow the ball. His burble expressed everybody's surprise. Willie Mackintosh had just put the ball in the net! And not just any old fashion, either. The ball had lifted and looped through the air and had seemed to *curve* into the corner of the goal. Noel picked it out – and tried again...

And again ... and again ... from all sorts of angles – from the corner flag, from a free kick in front of a wall of players... The ball dipped and curled nearly every time.

"He's Brazilian!" Mr Hooper gasped.

"He's Brazilliant!" laughed Noel, giving Willie a kiss.

"Whatever he is, you've cracked it, Noel. That player's a dead-ball specialist!"

Noel sat Willie on the table-top. "Set pieces," he beamed, remembering his dad's advice at the start of the match. "Say hello to my match-winning weapon, Dad."

"Hello," grinned Mr Hooper.

Burr-upp, went Slasher.

Chapter 8

A Star is Born

"*And welcome, everyone, to New Trufford Park, Munchester, for this fascinating clash between many people's favourites for the TFL crown, Munchester United, and those dogged northern raiders, Taggart's Tornados.*"

"Excuse me," Liam butted in tetchily. "*I'm* favourite for the title as I'm top of the league."

"Only on goal difference," Janice said softly.

"Wait till tomorrow," Liam promised darkly, when he was due to play Janice round at her house. "How do I zoom this camera again, Noel?"

"Button on the top," Noel said crossly, not wanting the distraction five minutes before kick-off. At the time, it had seemed like a great idea to have someone film his opening match. But with Liam at the controls, anything could happen. There would probably be shoes and curtains and bits of bedroom furniture all at wobbly angles on the video tomorrow.

"One of us two might be top o' the league, tonight," said Andy. He looked gingerly at Noel. Noel shrugged and smoothed out a crease in the pitch.

"*Yes*," Tim continued, "*a comprehensive victory for either of these teams could see them leading the pack by eight o'clock this evening. Top spot, of course, is presently held by Banana*

Rangers, who comfortably swept aside the gallant but slightly unlucky Weatherspoon Wanderers 3–0 on the opening night—"

"Unlucky?" Liam scoffed. "I was all over you." He focused the camera on Janice's knee.

"Oi!" she protested. "Watch where you're aiming that, Liam Watts!"

"*But whatever happens here,*" Tim went on regardless, "*it's all change tomorrow night when we visit the magnificent Pebble Lane Stadium to witness the keenly-awaited contest between Pebble Lane City and Banana Rangers. And to give us her views on how she thinks that match will go, I'm joined in the commentary box by the Pebble Lane manager, Janice 'Jumble' Sale.*"

"Thanks, Tim," said Janice. She turned and smiled gorgeously into Liam's lens. "Well, I think—"

"Anyone like a crumpet?" Noel's mum stuck her face round the bedroom door.

Liam panned his camera through a mobile on the ceiling, across Noel's posters and down into the doorway.

"Aw, don't record *this*," Noel groaned at Liam, sagging back on his heels in complete embarrassment. "Mum, do you mind? This is an important match. No one eats crumpets just before a big game."

"Only checking," she huffed, putting a hand across her face as she heard the sound of the camera zooming. "It's what mums do."

"Do it afterwards, then."

"Oh, charming. Thank you."

"How's he doing? How's he doing?" Noel heard his dad whisper from out on the landing.

"Losing, by the sound of it."

"We haven't STARTED yet!" Noel shouted angrily.

"Can I come in and watch?"

"NO! GET LOST!"

"Cheek! It was me who bought him the flippin' game, wasn't it?"

Noel kicked the door shut with a loudish bang.

"One minute to kick-off," Janice said sheepishly.

"Parents," Noel grumbled and spilled his players out on to the pitch.

"*And I'm afraid we'll have to leave that interview there*," said Tim, "*as the game looks just about ready to start. I'll run down the team-sheets in a moment. But I have to say first that's a dazzling strip that Munchester are wearing. What do you make of that, Janice?*"

"Well they didn't get it at a 'jumble sale', Tim."

"Ha ha," groaned Liam, and turned his camera on to Willie Mackintosh.

Tim recognized the movement right away. "*And there's the man they've all been talking about: Willie Mackintosh. Signed, of course, from Taggart's Tornados in the close season. How is he going to fare, tonight, one wonders? He's lining up wide on the left at the moment. Strange, we expected to see him adopt a much more central position, but no doubt Noel Hooper has his tactics well worked out.*"

He certainly has... thought Noel.

But it was as late as the nineteenth minute before anyone got to see them...

"*A minute to half-time,*" Tim commentated drily, "*in what's been a scrappy, uninteresting match. It's locked at 0–0 and neither side seems capable of taking the initiative. As for Mackintosh – well, we expected so much of him, but he's virtually been a passenger throughout the game.*"

"Very disappointing," Janice added.

"Looks like he's been super-glued to the touchline, Tim."

"*Anyway, the ball's with Twiggs,*" said Tim, getting slightly more animated as a gap opened up in Andy's defence. "*He tries to feed Buckham – but the ball's too long. Buckham chases it anyway. Doesn't make contact. MacRobbie hurries back to collect and – would you believe that? – chops Buckham down. Yellow card for MacRobbie from referee Weatherspoon. Free kick to Munchester on the left edge of the area.*"

"About time," said Liam, zooming in on the player in Noel's hands.

"Hooray," cheered Janice.

"*Well,*" Tim snorted into his microphone, "*the cheers you can hear are because, amazingly,* Mackintosh *has stepped forward to take the kick. He takes a moment or two to position himself. He looks like he might be trying to line up a shot. The angle's far too tight, surely? The Tornados aren't even bothering with a wall. Anyway, here it comes and – OH, I SAY! HOW DID THAT GET IN? IT SEEMED TO CURL RIGHT OUT OF MACDOUGALL'S REACH! THAT'S AN ASTONISHING STRIKE BY MACKINTOSH! THE CROWD ARE STUNNED INTO ABSOLUTE SILENCE. MANAGER MCTAGGART SHAKES HIS HEAD IN DISBELIEF AND I'M NOT SURPRISED! THAT HAS GOT TO BE THE GOAL OF THE SEASON SO FAR! And there goes the half-time whistle now. I can't wait to see a replay of that in the studio – over to you, Liam!*"

"Did you get it?" whooped Noel.

"That fluke?" said Liam.

"It didn't look fluky to me," said Janice. "How'd you do it, Noel? Can you give me a lesson?"

Noel looked up. Janice was smiling invitingly at him. Noel's stomach churned like a mini cement mixer. "Erm ... I ... need to go to the toilet, sorry."

Janice frowned in disappointment. Noel dashed from the room.

"*Noel Hooper keeping things close to his chest,*" said Tim, "*and who can blame him? Anyway, Mackintosh's goal has really sent a buzz around this crowd. Let's hope we see some more wizardry from the elusive front man in the second half...*"

And they did. Halfway through the second period, Noel forced another free kick directly in front of goal. It was a long way out but Andy McTaggart was taking no chances.

He built an eight-man wall and placed two men on the goal-line, hugging the posts. It made no difference. Willie Mackintosh scooped the ball up and bent it into the top left-hand corner. Andy's goalkeeper didn't even move. Everybody's mouth fell open in amazement.

"How does he *do* that?" Liam said.

No one knew – but Willie did it again thirty seconds from the end, this time from the penalty spot.

"*Clumsy tackle from McNugget,*" Tim blabbered. "*Still shell-shocked, no doubt, by those two incredible curlers from Mackintosh. And here's Mackintosh again, stepping up to take the penalty. In he comes now and... Yes! – it's there – as cool as an ice cube. MacDougall flung himself hard to his left but Mackintosh just said 'thank you very much' and plopped the ball into the centre of the goal! So confident it was*

almost flippant. That's *3–0, that's Mackintosh's hat trick, and* that *wraps up the points for Munchester United. They go joint top of the TFL. And there's a new star on the horizon tonight – his name is* WILLIE MACKINTOSH!"

Chapter 9

The Truth About Willie

"There, Dad," said Noel, "freeze it there!" He snatched the remote from his father's grasp and paused the video on a close-up of Janice. She was kneeling on the floor of Tim's attic room, her head propped up in the cup of her hands, her shining blue eyes intently following the return game between Taggart's Tornados and Munchester United. Noel let out an adoring sigh. Janice Jumble. She was just so...

"That's not Andy McTaggart," said Mr Hooper. "Move it on a bit, Noel. The interview must be after this."

"I think it's near here," Noel fibbed, using the excuse to advance the film a few frames at a time. A lock of brown hair fell in slow-motion across Janice's face. She blew it out of the way with a gentle, pouty movement of her lips. Noel blew her a little kiss.

"Give it here," said Mr Hooper irritably. He snatched the remote control back again and whizzed the video on a bit further. Subbuteo flashed by at nine times its normal speed. Then suddenly Mr Hooper put the video into normal play again and Tim Weatherspoon's voice came over the speakers:

"*Buckham, he does well to keep possession, but he doesn't seem to have too many options available—*"

"Exactly," Mr Hooper said, freezing the picture.

"Dad, this isn't Andy McTaggart, either."

"We'll get to his interview in a minute, Noel. Look at this picture first." Mr Hooper got down on his hands and knees, took out a marker pen and drew a circle on the screen around several players. Lately, the Hooper's TV set was beginning to resemble an Ordnance Survey map. Since the opening league fixtures a few weeks ago, Mr Hooper had been passionately studying videos of the games in order to advise Noel tactically on the best way of winning the championship. Noel had to admit, it had worked sometimes. It was his dad who had pointed out the weaknesses in Janice's play that had enabled Munchester United to grab the crucial 2–1 victory over Pebble Lane City that had seen them storm to the top of the league. Then again, his dad had also

advised playing a sweeper system against Liam – and Noel had lost that nail-biter 4–3. Things were getting very tight at the top. Noel glanced at the print-out of league positions lying on the floor in front of him...

Teams	Played	Won	Lost	Drawn	For	Against	Points	GD
Munchester United	6	4	1	1	18	7	13	+11
Pebble Lane City	7	4	2	1	19	9	13	+10
Banana Rangers	6	3	1	2	13	11	11	+2
Taggart's Tornados	6	1	2	3	10	11	6	–1
Weatherspoon Wanderers	7	0	6	1	2	24	1	–22

Remaining Fixtures:

Banana Rangers v Munchester Utd
Weatherspoon Wanderers v Taggart's Tornados

Banana Rangers v Taggart's Tornados
Pebble Lane City v Munchester Utd

Two games to go. Two tough ones as well. Defeat against Liam in tonight's match would be a disaster. Munchester United could still win the league but they had to face Pebble Lane City in their final game – while Liam's last match was against Andy McTaggart. Theoretically, Liam had the easier tie, but Andy had been playing a great deal better since Willie Mackintosh had thumped a hat trick past his gobsmacked Tornados several weeks earlier. In the return match, Noel had been lucky to escape with a 2–2 draw. But Liam could be unpredictable, too. He had arrogantly expected to slaughter Tim in *their* return match and had ended up conceding a 0–0 draw. The ball had hit every piece of plastic around Tim's goal, but Tim had still come away with a point. There was no telling what might happen in the next four games. Nevertheless, Noel was quietly confident.

"See," said Mr Hooper, rapping a knuckle on the screen. "Buckham and Roy Kleen are too far apart. And where's Nicky Blutt? Completely out of position. You've got to keep things much tighter, Noel. You need to win more midfield possession and give Twiggs more room out here..." he drew an arching arrow, "on the flanks."

"Yes, Dad," Noel nodded, forced to look up as Slasher padded in to see what was happening. The black cat brushed against Noel's thigh and promptly settled down on the sheet of league positions.

"Anyway," Mr Hooper said, "where's this interview you're so keen for me to see?" He whizzed the video on a bit further. The Subbuteo game came to a finish with Noel and Andy shaking hands. Then it was just Andy and Tim together, doing a post-match interview for the camera.

"*Andy, you must be gutted?*" asked Tim.

Andy gave a despairing nod. "*When we got the second goal I thought we had them, Tim. But we gave away a couple of silly fouls in the second period and you can't afford to do that with Mackintosh around.*"

"*He's lethal, isn't he?*"

"*Deadly, aye.*"

"*Could you have imagined before you sold him that he would possibly turn out as good as this?*"

Andy frowned and shook his head. "*Er no, not exactly.*"

"*Can you tell us what prompted you to sell him in the first place?*"

Andy shrugged. He turned his face away from the camera. The camera panned across the room. Janice was measuring Willie Mackintosh with a ruler and Noel was watching the interview.

"*Erm, well,*" said Andy. The camera jerked back, just in time to catch him

biting his lip. "*Actually, I thought he was jinxed, Tim.*"

"Jinxed?" Mr Hooper put the video on pause. "What's that supposed to mean?"

"Watch the next bit," said Noel, keeping a wary eye on Slasher. The cat was prowling about the floor, sniffing at the Subbuteo pitch and players. "You leave them, Slasher," Noel warned.

Ssss, went Slasher, and sat down to wash his tail.

"*Jinxed?*" On the video, Tim echoed Mr Hooper's concern.

"*Sort of ... accident prone,*" Andy explained sheepishly. "*It all started when he fell off the kitchen table and Mum ran him over with Melanie's pram.*"

"*You* what?" Noel's voice said, just off camera.

"*He must have suffered terrible*

injuries," said Tim. "*How long was he on the treatment table?*"

Andy gulped and turned tomato red. "*Not long, once I'd found all the bits...*"

"*Hhh,*" gasped Janice. "*I'm amazed he lived.*"

"*His body came out of his base,*" said Andy, "*and ... the dog ate it.*"

The picture shook as Liam hooted with laughter.

"*Ate it?*" Tim gulped. "*But how did you get him back again?*"

Andy bit his knuckles and glanced in Noel's direction. "*We had to wait until, y'know, the dog had done a pooh...*"

"*Ugh!*" went everyone, including Mr Hooper.

Burr-upp! went Slasher. Even he looked disgusted.

"That's horrible," Mr Hooper said. "I hope he disinfected him thoroughly

before he stuck him back together. Dog's pooh indeed. Yuk!"

"This is the important bit now," said Noel.

"*The thing is,*" Andy confessed, "*he wouldn't stand up right. He was all off-balance. So ... so I put a tiny pebble in his base.*"

"*That's why he doesn't spin right!*" Janice exclaimed off camera, which prompted the start of a long argument about the ethics of tampering with players and putting injured ones on the transfer market.

"Well," said Mr Hooper in a blustery tone. "All I can say is at least some justice has been done. How many goals has Willie got for you now?"

"Thirteen," replied Noel, still watching the video. Janice looked even prettier when she was angry. She had swept her hair back behind one ear and was giving Andy a serious telling-off. A funny tingle rolled along Noel's spine.

"Well at least he's in safe hands now," said Mr Hooper. "And if he does the business tonight against Liam, you're virtually guaranteed the championship, Noel."

"Umm," Noel grunted, staring dewy-eyed at Janice.

"Anyway, we'd better clear this stuff away before your mum gets in." Mr Hooper gathered up the Munchester squad and dropped them into a

Subbuteo box. "By the way, where did Slasher go?"

"Uh?" Noel grunted.

Mr Hooper looked at the TV screen. For the second time that day Janice's smiling face was frozen on it.

"Never mind," sighed Mr Hooper, "it's not important." He quietly fitted the lid on the box and left the game on the dining table.

Chapter 10

Disaster!

"*And here we are,*" said Tim, "*at Bread Pudding Park for this crucial clash between Banana Rangers and current league leaders, Munchester United. Earlier today, Taggart's Tornados continued their recent run of improved form by comfortably beating Weatherspoon Wanderers 4–2. That match had no real bearing on the championship – but this one definitely does. And it should be a cracker. On the last occasion these two teams met they produced a magnificent 7 goal thriller. The score, then, was 4–3 to Banana Rangers. If Rangers are to stay in the hunt for the title they simply must win tonight. Defeat or a draw would be no use at all. Manager Liam Watts looks reasonably confident as his yellow-shorted players take to the field, whereas Noel Hooper looks ... well, slightly bewildered. I wonder if we might get a quick comment from him? Problem, Noel?*"

"He's not here..." Noel murmured. "Willie's not here..."

"What?" gasped Janice, running her eye over Noel's players and rummaging around in his Subbuteo box. Andy McTaggart, on camera duty, panned the lens across Noel's forwards.

"Tough," sniffed Liam. "Come on, let's get on with it. This is gamesmanship, this is, ref."

"Shut up," said Janice, "this is serious. When did you last see him, Noel?"

Noel rubbed his brow in consternation. His flicking finger was trembling like mad. "He was in his box with the others," he mumbled. "But now..."

"*Sensational news!*" Tim Weatherspoon gabbled. "*Willie Mackintosh, the Munchester United star, failed to turn up for training this morning and hasn't been seen since—*"

"Shut up!" shouted Noel, as anger started to replace confusion. "He was in that box! Someone's STOLEN him!"

"Well don't look at ME," Liam defended angrily. "Who needs a player with a pebble in his base when you've got Danny Baggage?" He thrust an accusing finger at Janice. "*She's* the one who's been begging you for a transfer."

Janice blinked in shock and put a hand across her mouth. Noel frowned hard. Liam was right. Recently, Janice had offered to buy Willie Mackintosh for a Manchester United football annual. When Noel had refused to sell his star, Janice *had* got a bit huffy. But surely Janice wouldn't resort to theft?

"Liam Watts!" she retorted hotly, smacking Liam's shoulder so he grimaced in pain. "I have never stolen anything in my life, you creep!"

"Perhaps you just left him at home?" said a voice.

Everybody looked at the video camera. It bumped up and down as Andy shrugged his shoulders.

"Or perhaps you nicked him back," Noel snarled, "because he's scored five goals against you this season and you wished you hadn't sold him to me in the first place!"

"Get lost!" snapped Andy.

"Can we play now?" said Liam, looking at his watch.

"No!" Noel shouted, folding his arms. "I'm not playing without Willie. *Somebody*'s got him!"

Tim and Janice looked at one another. It was already two minutes past kick-off time. "Listen, Noel," said Janice soothingly, coming over and putting her arm around his shoulders. "Nobody here could have stolen Willie. No one had time. Perhaps you just forgot to put him in the box the last time you packed your players away?"

Noel hung his head in desperation. Then suddenly it struck him. Dad! Dad had put the players away that afternoon. Dad must have left Willie out of the box. "You're right!" He gave Janice a joyful look. "He must be at home! I'll nip back and fetch him!"

"Hang on," Liam protested, tapping

his watch. "It says in the rules that all matches will kick off on time. If Noel's late, I should be awarded the match."

"I'm the referee," Janice said haughtily. "I'll decide what happens, thank you."

"Huh," Liam snorted. "I don't think special favours are allowed just because the referee fancies the manager."

The room fell deathly silent. Janice went as red as a pepper. Noel kept his face down and pretended he was still looking for Willie Mackintosh.

"*Controversy here,*" Tim whispered quietly. "*Will referee Sale abandon the match? Will she ban Banana Rangers from the league? Will she whack Liam on the other shoulder? Will she—*"

"I have decided," Janice said imperiously, "that the game will begin."

"Aw, Jumble!"

"I'm sorry, Noel. Unfortunately, big mouth has got a point. It *is* time for kick-off. However, as these are difficult circumstances I'll allow you an extra five minutes at half-time to run home and fetch Willie—"

"Rubbish decision!" Liam barked.

Janice whipped out her yellow card.

"*Sensational,*" cried Tim. "*Liam Watts booked for foul and abusive language!*"

"Don't care," huffed Liam. "This game's ridiculous. She *wants* him to win!"

Janice's blue eyes flared. "*She* wants to win the league herself, *actually.*" She brought the whistle to her lips and blew it pertly. "Now kick off, both of you!"

"Or what?"

"Or else!"

Although Janice never specified what "or else" meant, Liam and Noel didn't argue further. The game began and soon turned into a real niggle match. Both teams committed a string of nasty fouls and Noel himself was booked by Janice over two hotly-disputed decisions. At half-time the score was a tense 0–0. As soon as the whistle blew, Noel flew home.

"Thought you were playing football?" said his mum as Noel crashed breathlessly into the kitchen.

"Where's Dad?"

"Working late tonight."

"Blast!" Noel dashed into the front. He pushed back the settee. Willie wasn't there. He checked under the sideboard. No players there, either. "Out the way!" he said to Slasher, pulling the fireside rug from under Slasher's paws.

Schstwswz! Frrsshhh! Rrrraowow! went Slasher. He took a swipe at Noel's ankle and fortunately missed.

Mrs Hooper walked into the lounge. "Noel? What on earth are you doing?"

"Oh, where *is* he?" Noel stamped, flinging cushions all over the room.

"Do you mind! I've just vacuumed in here, young man!"

Noel stopped flinging cushions. "The hoover," he said.

"Noel?" said his mother, as he darted towards the understairs cupboard. "Noel, what are you doing? Noel! DON'T YOU DARE EMPTY THAT HOOVER BAG OUT IN THE HALL!"

But it was too late. A light grey cloud of dust and hair and bits of gubbins had already exploded on the hall carpet. But there was no Willie Mackintosh hidden in the mess. Noel's shoulders drooped. He kicked the hoover in blind frustration then opened the latch and stormed out of the front door leaving it swinging. For a second, Mrs Hooper was just too stunned to speak.

"AND WHERE DO YOU THINK YOU'RE GOING?" she eventually roared.

"Liam's," growled Noel, and punched a fist into the hedge as he passed.

Janice met him at the door to Liam's house. Noel looked at her, gulped and shook his head. As he entered Liam's bedroom he snapped at Andy who aimed his camera lens on to the pitch. Liam folded his arms and tapped his foot. Tim made one or two speculative remarks about the possibility of Willie being kidnapped by aliens. Then Janice

blew her whistle and the second half began. Tim reminded his "listeners" of the importance of the game and how the loss of Mackintosh had badly affected Munchester's morale. He was right – Noel's heart was simply not in it. Early in the second half, Danny Baggage broke the deadlock with a soft, deflected goal that squirmed in off a post. Liam punched the air in delight. Noel substituted his goal-keeper in disgust. When the final whistle sounded he packed up his players, said nothing to anyone and mooched off home.

He had lost 4–0.

And Banana Rangers were top of the league.

Teams	Played	Won	Lost	Drawn	For	Against	Points	GD
Banana Rangers	7	4	1	2	17	11	14	+6
Pebble Lane City	7	4	2	1	19	9	13	+10
Munchester United	7	4	2	1	18	11	13	+7
Taggart's Tornados	7	2	2	3	14	13	9	+1
Weatherspoon Wanderers	8	0	7	1	4	28	1	–24

Remaining Fixtures:

Banana Rangers v Taggart's Tornados
Pebble Lane City v Munchester Utd

Chapter 11

Ouch!

Two nights after his disastrous defeat, Noel received a couple of unexpected visitors. His mum was the one who answered the door.

"Hello, Mrs Hooper," Janice said shyly.

Tim Weatherspoon added, "Is Noel in, please?"

"Well now, I'm not really sure," said Mrs Hooper, propping a finger under her chin. "There's certainly some creature that *looks* like Noel floating around the upstairs rooms. It doesn't eat very much or make much mess and it's ever so, EVER so good at dusting. If you ask me, it's a zombie – but you can go up and check for yourselves if you like."

"I think we'd better," said Janice, sounding concerned.

"One moment." Mrs Hooper raised a hand. Tim and Janice paused at the foot of the stairs. Mrs Hooper dipped into the understairs cupboard and handed them both a duster each. "You'll find those useful," she said with a giggle, and went into the lounge la-la-ing to herself.

"This is worse than I thought," said Janice. With a flick of her hair she pounded up the stairs.

They found Noel in the bathroom, dusting shampoo bottles. "Go away," he muttered without looking up.

"We've come to help you find Willie Mackintosh," said Tim.

"Don't wanna find Willie flipping Mackintosh, *thank you.*"

"Yes you do," said Janice softly. "Erm, why are you dusting bathcubes, Noel?"

Noel told them about the hoover bag and how his punishment was to dust every reachable surface in the house.

"Bad," said Janice with a sympathetic nod. She pushed up her sleeves. "Right, I'll do the shower rail. Tim, you do the linen basket..."

Half an hour later, when the bathroom was done and all three had been down on their hands and knees and combed every inch of the Hooper's front room, there was still no sign of the missing superstar.

"Think hard," said Janice, gently beating a cushion on the floor. "Who

else came into the room besides you and your dad?"

"No one," said Noel. "We just watched Andy's interview then Dad packed up the players and that was it."

Tim frowned thoughtfully and looked at Janice. "Noel," she said, "how well do you know your dad?"

"What?" said Noel.

"Can you trust him?" asked Tim.

"What?" said Noel again. He was getting neck-ache twisting his head from side to side.

Janice moved a bit closer. Their shoulders touched. Her soft brown hair fell across Noel's hand. He pulled away nervously as if he'd been burned. "Your dad likes Subbuteo, doesn't he?"

"Yeah, but—"

"And you always beat him, don't you?"

"Yeah—"

"What if he was jealous of you?"

"What if he was jealous of *Willie*?" hissed Tim, shuffling up like a human book-end.

There was a pause. Noel answered: "What if he was?"

"Doh!" Janice thumped him hard in the chest. "He'd steal him, you idiot. So the next time you played, he'd have a chance of beating you."

"It's the only explanation," Tim said seriously. "It's your dad, Noel. He's the culprit. He's got to be the one who kidnapped Willie..."

Just then, Mr Hooper walked into the lounge. "Hi kids," he said.

Janice, Noel and Tim exchanged scornful glances. "Get him!" shouted Janice and they leapt on Mr Hooper and pinned him to the carpet...

"OK, OK. So now you have to tidy up the garage as well," said Janice, slicing green beans into a

saucepan. "It's not the end of the world, Noel."

"It was worth a try," Tim said encouragingly, sliding a plate out of the washing-up bowl.

"You're both mental," said Noel, flopping down on a stool. Not surprisingly, his dad had denied abducting Willie and had heaped the garage punishment on top of the dusting. It hadn't helped that Noel's mum had walked in just as they were shining a desk lamp in Mr Hooper's face either. She had promptly aided her husband's rescue by dragging Tim and Janice off in a flash and giving them jobs to do in the kitchen. It was all going horribly, horribly wrong – and still Willie Mackintosh had not been found.

Over tea, everyone except Mr and Mrs Hooper was silent. "Lovely beans," Mr Hooper noted.

"On such nice clean plates as well," said his wife.

Noel tutted and tried to saw through the end of one of the burnt sausages he'd been made to cook for him and his "delightful" friends (Mrs Hooper's description). When the sausage wouldn't give, he whacked it noisily with the edge of his knife and sent the end shooting off his plate and on to the floor.

"Pick that up," his mother said calmly.

"Then wash the fluff off and eat it," said his dad.

Noel slammed down his knife and bent to get the sausage. "Can't," he said. "Slasher's got it."

"What have I told you about feeding that cat at mealtimes?" Mrs Hooper scolded. "Oh well, I suppose if Slasher's got it, it's best to let him have it. I wish he wouldn't take it to his dustbin, though. I dread to think what else he's stuffed away in there..."

"DUSTBIN!" Noel sat up so fast he bumped his head on the underside of the table. The one place he hadn't searched: Slasher's dustbin.

"Noel?" said Mr Hooper as Noel leapt down and crawled on his hands and knees up to Slasher's door. "Noel, what are you doing? Noel, be careful."

"Give him back," Noel growled. "I know you've got him!"

Ssss! went Slasher, flattening his ears.

"Noel?" said Mrs Hooper, looking rather anxious. "Don't do anything rash, now, will you...?"

It was like something out of a horror movie. As Noel thrust his hand in and felt around, Slasher lashed out with his powerful claws. Noel screamed. Slasher hissed. Noel screamed again. Mr Hooper fainted. Slasher yowled. Janice covered her eyes. Mrs Hooper bit her knuckles. Tim ate his sausage and tried to tell himself it wasn't really happening.

But it was. Slasher was the culprit. He was the one who had stolen Willie. Wincing with pain, Noel reached up and dropped his player on the dining table. Willie wobbled slightly and parted from his base. And it was only then that Janice saw the extent of Noel's injuries.

"Hhh!" she gasped. "Look at your hand!"

Several deep scratches were gouged in Noel's flesh.

Blood was pouring from his flicking finger...

Chapter 12

The Final Fixture

"But you *can't* play," said Janice, examining Noel's hand. "It looks worse than it did when Slasher first got you."

"It's very swollen," Tim remarked.

"Did you have to have a tetanus jab?" asked Andy.

"In your bum?" asked Liam, training the camera on the scabby finger. It was four days now since Willie's rescue. Noel's finger looked worse than one of his cooked sausages, but he was determined to play Janice – and win the title.

"It only hurts if I bend it back too far. I want to play. So does Willie..."

Willie Mackintosh, like Noel, had spent time on the "treatment table" himself. After the rescue Mr Hooper had super-glued him back together, but in the process had dislodged the pebble from his base. There was no telling which way up the pebble should have been and because Noel had been too poorly to train, it was difficult to know whether Willie retained his ability to curve the ball properly or not.

"Well, I think it's daft," Janice said, crossing her arms. "In my opinion, Noel's not fit. I think we should either postpone the game or declare it void and make Liam champion."

That produced a barrage of protests all round.

Andy McTaggart blew the match whistle. "As the referee, I say if Noel thinks he's all right the game goes ahead."

All the boys nodded in agreement.

"Stupid decision," Janice muttered.

But a few minutes later, the game was under way...

"*This is it!*" Tim cried. "*The match that everyone's been waiting for, the game that must decide the TFL crown. Amazingly, Banana Rangers squandered their chance of becoming outright winners of the TF League when they went down 6–4 to the vastly improved Taggart's Tornados earlier today...*"

"Hmph," muttered Janice. "Liam Watts was thinking about Rule 10 if you ask me."

"*So referee McTaggart blows the whistle – and we're away! Munchester United straight on to the attack!*

Buckham feeds Blutt. He's blocked by a wall of Pebble Lane players but manages to bundle the ball through to Twiggs. Twiggs stumbles down the line and misses his kick completely. Cartwright slides across to gather the ball and, oh dear, pumps it straight into touch. Early signs of nerves from both these teams..."

"Come on..." Janice muttered, "concentrate."

"*Blutt with the throw. Scrambled forward by Kleen. Intercepted by Jefferson on the edge of the area. He tries to flick the ball upfield to Court but makes a dreadful hash of it! The ball's rolled straight to the feet of Mackintosh! Mackintosh shoots and ...*

ohhh, it's clipped the angle of the bar and post! What a let-off that was for Pebble Lane City. Janice Sale heaves a sigh of relief. Noel Hooper throws his head back and covers his face. He knows that was a golden opportunity to snatch an early lead. Could it be that Mackintosh is still feeling the effects of being held hostage in a dustbin all week?"

"Well, that shot was certainly rubbish," muttered Liam.

"*Now Pebble Lane come bursting forward themselves, piling pressure on the Munchester defence. Cartwright slips a lovely pass forward to Rain who ... oops, can't control it and loses possession immediately to Buckham. There could be a break on here for Munchester. It's four against two. Buckham whacks the ball upfield and finds ... MACKINTOSH ALONE WITH A SHOOTING CHANCE!*

Crumley comes out to narrow the angle! Mackintosh hits it and ooh ... it curls well wide of the post. Dear, oh dear. He really should have put that chance away..."

"Oh, what's the matter with you?" Noel tutted, repositioning Willie for another goal kick.

"*Two scoring opportunities gone begging,*" Tim burbled, "*and there might be a chance for a third one here as Crumley fluffs his goal kick straight to Blutt. Blutt knocks it on to Twiggs who barges through ... and SCORES! GREAT INDIVIDUAL GOAL BY TWIGGS! – but wait, what's this? The referee's shaking his head.*"

"Offside," said Andy McTaggart.

"No way!" cried Noel, looking down at his players. "Twiggs ran past the last defender!"

"It was Mackintosh," said Liam,

zooming in on the evidence. "He's just in front of Jumble's back four."

"Ohhh, Willie!" Noel cried, and banged his fist down hard. A floodlight stand toppled on to the pitch and a photographer figure fell off the table. But despite the manager's angry outburst, Mackintosh's form did not improve. Twice more he sent chances whistling over the Pebble Lane bar and the half finished exactly as it had started: goal-less.

"*Mackintosh is having a stinker,*" Tim remarked.

His manager couldn't have put it better.

To make matters worse, Noel's finger was throbbing like a nuclear reactor. At half-time he went to the kitchen to dunk it into a beaker of ice. As he wandered back up the hall, he heard Janice giving her team a half-time lecture...

"You're playing like a bunch of plastic pegs! We could have been 5–0 down by now! What's happened to the cover at the back? Mackintosh has had so much space he could have pitched a tent in our penalty area. Wake up! I want to see more fight, more commitment and more shots in this half! Court, take a bath. Chestikov, you're on. It's time to prove you're worth that bar of fruit and nut chocolate I paid for you. Now get in there the lot of you and get this game won!"

"*Well, I don't know what was said in the dressing-room,*" gushed Tim, "*but the home team have started this second half looking like their shorts are on fire! Bulgarian maestro Ivor Chestikov has already displayed some fine touches and he's here again now, chipping the ball through to Cartwright. Back again to Chestikov, who spreads it wide to*

Rain. Mackintosh comes hurrying down the line, but tussles with Rain and gives away a free kick in a dangerous position. Pebble Lane take their time about this. They've got their big men forward – three, four, five in the box. Are we going to see a chip to the far side for Nicely? No, it's a decoy! Rain taps it short to Chestikov who drills it low through a ruck of players and ... IT'S THERE! IT'S GONE IN! IT TOOK A CRUEL DEFLECTION OFF A MUNCHESTER PLAYER, BUT CHESTIKOV IS CLAIMING IT! THE NEW SIGNING HAS SCORED! HE RUNS TO THE CORNER FLAG TO DO A LITTLE SHIMMY AS MANAGER SALE DOES A CART-WHEEL FOR THE CAMERAS! What an inspired substitution that was. Some Munchester players are busy complaining that they were still organizing their wall when the kick was taken, but the referee is waving their protests away. The goal stands and Pebble Lane City are ahead. Now, what have Munchester got left in the locker?"

"A smelly pair of trainers last time I looked," said Liam, focusing on Janice's wild-haired, celebratory rave.

"Get lost, Watts," Noel snapped.

"Any more of that and I'll book you," said Andy.

"Hmph!" went Noel, and bad-temperedly plonked his men down for the kick-off.

Meanwhile, Janice was placing her men very precisely. She had tightened up her game considerably in the second half and was causing Noel plenty of problems up front. "Just keep up the pressure," she told her team. But as she glanced across the room and saw the TFL trophy glinting like an untouched jewel on the window-sill, her stomach

took a twist and she breathed in hard. And that was when the nerves began to creep in...

"*Buckham,*" snorted Tim, "*coming forward yet again. Desperately searching for this equalizing goal. He skips past Rain but – oh, is cynically hacked down by Jefferson. That's a red card for Jefferson – sent to his box for his third bad foul in as many minutes. There's no doubt about it, Pebble Lane City are beginning to crack as Munchester heap the pressure on late. You really sense there might be something in this game for them yet.*"

"Come on-nn," Noel told himself, blowing cool air over his fingers. They were beginning to hurt him badly again. But he had to keep going. Tim was right. Janice was on edge. He took the free kick.

"*Buckham chips it into the area,*" said Tim. "*Cartwright knocks it out –*

but only as far as Twiggs! Twiggs shoots! Crumley gets down and parries it away! It comes to Blutt who fires in a low cross which Crumley punches out to the wing. Kleen is there, to set up Buckham. Buckham with a scorcher! Off the underside of the bar! DID IT CROSS THE LINE?!"

"No," said Liam, from behind the camera.

"Play on," said Andy.

"Help," Janice whimpered, frantically

waving her goalkeeper at the ball and dibbling it out – to the feet of Willie Mackintosh...

"*Desperate moments!*" Tim Weatherspoon cried. "*Surely this pressure must pay off? The ball's with Mackintosh! He's lining up the shot!*"

"Oh no," muttered Janice, "not Mackintosh, not now..." and she threw Nigel Crumley at Willie's effort.

"*INCREDIBLE!*" screamed Tim. "*HOW DID CRUMLEY GET HIS FINGERTIPS TO THAT?*"

"Corner," said Andy.

"I saved it," Janice squeaked. "I saved a Mackintosh special!"

"Fff," Noel blustered, hastily flicking players into Janice's area. Janice, in turn, brought everyone except Alan Nicely back. Noel picked Willie Mackintosh up. Maybe if Willie could deliver a good cross, someone could nod it into the net? He got down and prepared to take the corner, his flicking finger throbbing like crazy. He was convinced now that his injury was the reason why Willie had mistimed so many of his shots. And then, suddenly, a clever thought struck him. Why not use his other hand? It was a tricky proposition, but anything was worth a try this late in the game...

"*Mackintosh with ... a* left-footed *corner?*" Tim queried. "*This is something we haven't seen before ... here it comes anyway and...*"

"CRIKEY, IT'S IN!" Liam shouted out loud, nearly toppling over backwards in his excitement. "DIRECT FROM A CORNER! How'd he manage that?"

"Don't know," said Noel, scrambling his players back into his half, "but let's get on with it, there can't be long left."

"One minute," said Andy.

"Stay cool, Jumble," Liam said. "Even if you draw you'll still win the league on goal difference."

Janice bit her lip. "Umm, stay cool," she nodded to herself – and promptly gave the ball away straight from the kick-off.

"*Blue shirts SURGING forward,*" yelped Tim. "*This has* got *to be Munchester's very last chance! Buckham, so often the Munchester mastermind, knocks it wide to Twiggs. Twiggs brings it inside, tries a weak-looking shot which Crumley flaps at*

and fumbles round the post. Janice Sale is hopping mad. She knows that shot was going wide and Crumley could have safely left it. Now Pebble Lane have to face another corner – and guess who's stepping up to take it?"

"Come on, Willie," Noel told his star. "Just like before. Curl it straight in." He piled every player into Janice's area again, even his goalkeeper Peter Schmuckle. Janice left Chestikov and Alan Nicely up.

"*The whole ground holds its breath,*" gasped Tim, "*as Mackintosh shapes up for another in-swinger! It's another beauty – but this time Crumley gets his hands to it and manages to punch it away from danger! It's ... it's rolling upfield ... straight to Chestikov. He turns on a penny and knocks it on to Nicely ... the Munchester defence are all upfield! They haven't a hope of*

getting back in time. All Nicely has to do is tap it in the net!"

"I can't," said Janice, pulling her finger away. "It's too easy."

"Ten seconds," said Andy.

"*Nicely's stuck in the mud!*" yelled Tim.

Janice looked at the distraught Noel. "It's not fair," she said, "you've played really well."

"You've still won," said Liam, "put it in, anyway."

"Three seconds," said Andy.

"I'll blast it over the bar," said Janice.

And promptly blasted it into the roof of the net.

Chapter 13

The Champion

"We're thrilled," sniffed Janice into Tim Weatherspoon's mike, "honestly we are, Tim. Over the moon. Happy as hamsters. We're really..."

"Crikey, she sounds it," Liam muttered to Andy as joyous tears flooded down Janice's cheeks. She displayed the TFL trophy for the camera and Liam, dutifully, recorded her victory.

"*Emotional scenes here at Pebble*

Lane," said Tim, "*as Janice Sale gathers up her victorious players and does a lap of honour round her impressive stadium...*"

"Slow down," complained Liam, trying to follow Janice round, "you're making me dizzy! Jumble, slow down."

"*So let's take a final look at the table,*" said Tim, grabbing hold of Liam and making him focus on the sheet of paper in his hand.

Teams	Played	Won	Lost	Drawn	For	Against	Points	GD
Pebble Lane City	8	5	2	1	21	10	16	+11
Banana Rangers	8	4	2	2	21	17	14	+4
Munchester United	8	4	3	1	19	13	13	+6
Taggart's Tornados	8	3	2	3	20	17	12	+3
Weatherspoon Wanderers	8	0	7	1	4	28	1	–24

"*Thanks to that bizarre late goal from Nicely, Pebble Lane City finish as outright champions on 16 points. But it was tremendously tight at the end.*

Any of the top three teams could have won it. The unluckiest side of all has to be Munchester United, plagued by injuries so late in the season. And the player of the season? Well, there's surely only one candidate. Join us later for a special compilation programme featuring the outstanding goals of Willie Mackintosh. Who will ever forget his blistering skills...?"

"Me," said a voice on the far side of the room. Noel was sitting quietly in a corner holding Willie Mackintosh in the palm of his hand. He looked up as everybody turned towards him. "I'd like to make an announcement, Tim."

Tim walked over and thrust the microphone under Noel's nose.

Noel cleared his throat and announced very slowly: "Willie Mackintosh has just put in a transfer request..."

* * *

"WHAT?" screeched Mr Hooper when Noel broke the news. "You've sold him? You've sold your BEST PLAYER?"

A-roww? went Slasher, twizzling his ears. He gave Noel a look of deep disgust, jumped down off the sofa and slinked out of the room.

Mr Hooper put a hand against Noel's brow. "Are you feeling all right? Shall I call your mum? Maybe Slasher poisoned your brain when he scratched you? You can't sell Mackintosh. He's your star. You can't do it, Noel. It's sheer madness."

"I've done it, Dad. So there. I got a good deal for him. I sold him to—"

"I'm sure you got a *very* good deal," said Mr Hooper, pacing the room in exasperation. "He's worth more than everybody else's team put together. Was it because you had to use your left hand? All we need to do is unglue him

again and fix the pebble back with the weight to the right, then everything will be back to normal."

Noel shook his head.

Mr Hooper went "Agh!" and tugged at his hair. "But *why*, Noel? Why get rid of Mr Brazilliant?"

"Because," said Noel, opening a comic, "next season, I want to prove I can win matches without a freak player. I want to do it on my own, Dad. I want to win the league properly so that ... so that Janice will be proud of me..."

Mr Hooper slapped a hand against his brow. "I thought you'd been mooning over her for a while. I hope you didn't throw that last match, Noel? There's more to life than girls, you know. I thought she was sweet on Liam Watts anyway?"

"No," said Noel, in a prickly voice. "She's *mad* at Liam, now. She hates his

guts. We had a rule that said if Liam won the league he had to take Janice out to the pictures..."

Mr Hooper raised an eyebrow.

"...and when Janice said to him, 'Well, at least you don't have to go on a date with me now, Liam', Liam said he wouldn't have done *anyway*. And Janice started to cry. So ... so ... I said *I'd* take Janice to the pictures – if she wanted to go..."

"Very noble of you. Did she accept?"

Noel closed his comic and picked at the scabs on his injured finger. "She was *going* to, she *was* ... until *Tim* stood up and said he hadn't seen *Dinosaur Danger* yet. He said *he'd* like to take Janice out as well. And then Andy sort of shoved Tim out of the way and said he'd already seen *Dinosaur Danger* and it was rubbish, and then *he* asked Janice if she wanted to come to his house and watch a video..."

"Popular girl," Mr Hooper muttered.

"Then Liam stuck a finger in Andy's chest and said if *anyone* was going to take Janice to the pictures or show her a video it was *him*, because *he'd* only been kidding and Janice liked him the best, anyway..."

"Then what happened?"

"We all started to fight."

"Good grief." Mr Hooper covered his eyes. "Fancy, fighting over a girl!"

"She's not just 'a girl'," Noel said hotly. "She's the TFL champion – she's pretty, too."

Mr Hooper just sighed. "So, you lot ended up in disgrace and poor old Janice didn't get her date after all?"

Noel shuffled uncomfortably in his seat. "Not exactly. She said as she was the one who'd won the league it ought to be up to her to decide who she wanted to go to the pictures with."

"And?" said Mr Hooper. "Don't keep me in suspense. Which of you did she choose to go with...?"

"You'll like this," giggled Janice. "It's a much better film than *Dinosaur Danger*. It's about a man who's trapped in a boy's body – it's quite appropriate really..."

"Shush!" went a voice in the seats behind her.

"Shush yourself," said Janice. "Don't mind them," she whispered to her date. "They're probably just jealous. Do you want some ice-cream? Taste mine if

you like? Or some popcorn? This strawberry flavour is really good."

"Shush!" said the voice again, even more insistent.

"Get lost!" snapped Janice, over her shoulder. "Leave us alone."

"Us?" a voice whispered. "What's she mean, 'us'?"

"Ooh, look!" Janice shouted, bouncing in her seat. "An advert for Subbuteo!" She cupped her hands round her mouth and shouted: "Pebble Lane are champions!"

The whole cinema went "Shush!"

Janice stuck out her tongue – then hastily stuffed some popcorn in her mouth, just as an usherette came to investigate. "Excuse me, young lady, can you keep your voice down, please? The film's about to start. There are lots of people queuing as well – is that seat next to you taken?"

"Yes!" said Janice, sitting bolt upright.

"Are you sure?" The usherette aimed her torch. "I can't see any coats on it."

"It's taken," said Janice in a stiff, defensive tone. She glanced at the tiny figure beside her, staring blankly at the cinema screen. "I'll protect you," she whispered, "you're a Pebble Lane player now." She slipped a hand round Willie Mackintosh's base. "Champi-uns..." she sang quietly, stroking Willie's back. And as the lights went down she allowed herself to dream – of the goals and the glory and the shining trophies next season's TFL was sure to bring...

Elizabeth Lindsay

Ride into adventure with Mory and her pony, Midnight Dancer

Book 1: Midnight Dancer
Mory is thrilled when she finds the perfect pony. But will she be allowed to keep her?

Book 2: Midnight Dancer: To Catch a Thief
There's a thief with his eye on Mory's mother's sapphire necklace – and it's down to Mory and Midnight Dancer to save the day...

Book 3: Midnight Dancer: Running Free
Mory and Dancer have a competition to win. But they also have a mystery to solve...

Book 4: Midnight Dancer: Fireraisers
There's trouble on Uncle Glyn's farm – because there's a camper who loves playing with fire. Can Mory and Dancer avert disaster?

Book 5: Midnight Dancer: Joyriders
Mory's rival, Caroline, has her twin cousins to stay. And they look like trouble...

Book 6: Midnight Dancer: Ride By Night
Sheep are disappearing from the hillsides, and Mory and Midnight Dancer are determined to help...

HIPPO GHOST

Secrets from the past... Danger in the present...
Hippo Ghost brings you the spookiest of tales...

Castle of Ghosts
Carol Barton
Abbie's *bound* to see some ghosts at the castle where her aunt works – isn't she?

The Face on the Wall
Carol Barton
Jeremy knows he must solve the mystery of the face on the wall – however much it frightens him...

Summer Visitors
Carol Barton
Emma thinks she's in for a really boring summer, until she meets the Carstairs family on the beach. But there's something very *strange* about her new friends...

Ghostly Music
Richard Brown
Beth loves her piano lessons. So why have they started to make her *ill*...?

A Patchwork of Ghosts
Angela Bull
Who is the evil-looking ghost tormenting Lizzie, and why does he want to hurt her...?

The Ghosts who Waited
Dennis Hamley
Everything's changed since Rosy and her family moved house. Why has everyone suddenly turned against her...?

The Railway Phantoms

Dennis Hamley

Rachel has visions. She dreams of two children in strange, disintegrating clothes. And it seems as if they are trying to contact her. . .

The Haunting of Gull Cottage

Tessa Krailing

Unless Kezzie and James can find what really happened in Gull Cottage that terrible night many years ago, the haunting may never stop. . .

The Hidden Tomb

Jenny Oldfield

Can Kate unlock the mystery of the curse on Middleton Hall, before it destroys the Mason family. . . ?

The House at the End of Ferry Road

Martin Oliver

The house at the end of Ferry Road has just been built. So it can't be haunted, can it. . . ?

Beware! This House is Haunted
This House is Haunted Too!

Lance Salway

Jessica doesn't believe in ghosts. So who *is* writing the strange, spooky messages?

The Children Next Door

Jean Ure

Laura longs to make friends with the children next door. But they're not quite what they seem. . .

The Girl in the Blue Tunic

Jean Ure

Who is the strange girl Hannah meets at school – and why does she seem so alone?

HIPPO ANIMAL

Have you ever longed for a puppy to love, or a horse of your own? Have you ever wondered what it would be like to make friends with a wild animal? If so, then you're sure to fall in love with these fantastic titles from Hippo Animal!

Owl Cry

Deborah van der Beek

Can Solomon really look after an abandoned baby owl?

Thunderfoot

Deborah van der Beek

When Mel finds the enormous, neglected horse Thunderfoot, she doesn't know it will change her life for ever…

Vanilla Fudge

Deborah van der Beek

When Lizzie and Hannah fall in love with the same dog, neither of them will give up without a fight…

A Foxcub Named Freedom

Brenda Jobling

An injured vixen nudges her young son away from her. She can sense danger and cares nothing for herself – only for her son's freedom…

Goose on the Run

Brenda Jobling

It's an unusual pet – an injured Canada goose. But soon Josh can't imagine being without him. And the goose won't let *anyone* take him away from Josh...

Pirate the Seal

Brenda Jobling

Ryan's always been lonely – but then he meets Pirate and at last he has a real friend...

Animal Rescue

Bette Paul

Can Tessa help save the badgers of Delves Wood from destruction?

Take Six Kittens

Bette Paul

James and Jenny's dad promises them a pet when they move to the country. But they end up with more than they bargained for...

Take Six Puppies

Bette Paul

Anna knows she shouldn't get attached to the six new puppies at the Millington Farm Dog Sanctuary, but surely it can't hurt to get just a *little* bit fond of them...